SEX AT WORK COLLECTION

EXPLICIT DIRTY EROTICA SHORT STORIES

HELANA PARKINS

plicit Press
Erotica Fiction

CHAPTER 1

GINN'S BAD APPLE

TWENTY-FOUR-YEAR-OLD GINN MILTON had a thing for bad boys. When she saw Rollin Thorne, the thirty-year-old dad of the fifth-grader, Dean, she knew she had to fuck him. He had thick hair the color of caramel, and silver-gray eyes that could look right through a person. He was just above six feet and had a lean body that moved like liquid sex. Ginn shivered. She was wet just thinking about him and imagining what lay beneath those sinfully tight t-shirts and hung-just-right jeans he always wore. She wondered if those long fingers meant what she hoped. He missed the fall parent-teacher conferences.

She had been waiting for any reason to call him in. When Dean had turned in a plagiarized book report, she'd had the perfect excuse.

With her bright red hair and dark gray eyes, Ginn always received her fair share of attention from her students' families; male, female, married, divorced, it didn't matter. Ginn refused to encourage the married ones – unless, of course, the wife wanted to join in. She was all for experimentation and broadening her horizons.

Rollin, however, had never once made a pass, his cool gaze just flicking over her slender form with apparent disinterest. Tonight, she was determined to crack that icy exterior. She'd arranged for Rollin to come in late, claiming a tutoring session, but in reality, she hadn't wanted to risk anyone interrupting. The danger was part of the fun, but Ginn wasn't completely reckless.

She sat on the edge of her chair, ears straining for the sound of footsteps echoing in the empty corridors. She'd barely been able to concentrate all day, nipples hard and aching, and cunt wet and eager to be filled. She'd actually given in to her students' pleas to go outside at the end of the day, hoping the unseasonably warm late autumn air would distract her.

It hadn't worked.

The knock at the door made her jump. "Come in," she called, keeping her voice low and even. Only after she'd glimpsed the familiar profile did she turn and give Rollin the full view of her outfit.

"Miss Milton?" The question in his very tone was the first indication that she was going to get what she wanted.

Ginn uncrossed her legs, giving Rollin a glimpse of her freshly waxed pussy. His eyes widened, the lust darkening them as they ran up her body to the fitted white blouse that she'd left unbuttoned down to her sternum. Her breasts were on the small side, but that meant she could forgo a bra and no one really noticed. Unless, of course, she happened to be wearing a nearly see-through shirt that clearly showed the outlines of her pale pink nipples.

Rollin blinked and the swagger was back. He took

several steps forward, his body rolling gracefully, almost feline in its movements. The only lingering evidence of his previous change in expression was the heat in his eyes.

"Your son has been a very bad boy," Ginn took her ruler between her fingers. "Does he get that from you?" She ran the edge of it along her bottom lip.

Two more steps and he was there. He nudged her knees apart to move even closer. His eyes locked with hers and his hand closed around the ruler. His other hand made short work of his buckle and zipper. Ginn made an appreciative noise as Rollin's cock emerged, half-hard, easily seven inches already, and growing even more as she watched.

Rollin dug his fingers into her thick hair and pulled her head towards his waiting dick. Ginn opened her mouth, eagerly taking in the thick shaft. He didn't let her set the pace. In fact, she barely had time to get her hands on his hips before he began fucking her face. Or, more accurately, forcing her to use her mouth to fuck him.

Ginn's eyes teared up with every yank on her hair, breath coming in fits and starts as his cock swelled, filling her mouth. Just when it was almost too much, when the head of his dick was bumping the back of her throat and her jaw was starting to ache, he yanked her off, the swollen member popping from between her lips with an obscene sound.

With his hand still gripping her hair, he pulled Ginn to her feet and spun her around to bend her over her desk. He leaned over her, chest warm against her back, erection hard against her cloth-covered ass. "Pull up your skirt." The words sent a chill down Ginn's spine but, as soon as Rollin stepped back, she did as he said and flipped up the back of her skirt.

The crack came a second before the sting and Ginn jumped, gasping. Rollin stared down at her, the offending ruler in his left hand. She blinked but didn't protest or look away. The next blows came in rapid succession, each hard enough to draw a noise from Ginn, but none enough to make her stop. She whimpered as his hand caressed one throbbing cheek, palm cool against her hot flesh.

She felt the head of his cock brush her entrance and instantly knew what was coming next. She'd known from the first moment she'd decided to do this that he would take control now, and she surrendered herself to it. She came the second he penetrated her, the days and hours of fantasies exploding through her mind as he filled her, stretching her wide around him, the burning in her cheeks fading into the background.

He set a bruising pace, hips snapping forward with enough force to drive the air from her lungs and turn her cries into breathless whimpers. Her nipples chafed against her shirt and his fingers dug into her hips hard enough that she knew she'd have bruises. Every sensation was intensified as it raced across her nerves, pain, and pleasure mixing into one constant, overwhelming orgasm that had her limp and boneless even as he kept fucking her. Just as the pleasure threatened to turn into pain, Rollin buried himself deep with a grunt and came.

Ginn hissed as he pulled out half a minute later, his cum running down her leg. She heard his zipper but still didn't quite have the energy to move. She felt completely and thoroughly fucked. Rollin brushed back a few strands of hair and she looked up at him.

"Dean will have a new report on your desk on Monday," a smile played across his full lips. "But feel free to call me any time you feel like he's being... bad."

It was several minutes before Ginn was able to stand and straighten her clothes. Now she was really glad she'd asked him to come in on a Friday. After that fucking, she wasn't going to be able to sit down for a while. Not, she smiled, that she really minded. The parents were the best part of teaching.

CHAPTER 2

AISLE 69

IT WAS GETTING LATE on Friday night at the Sack and Bag grocery store in Springfield, Missouri. I work here, and I knew when it got to be close to eleven p.m. It was almost time for the regular store to close and for us stockers to hit the shelves. I was the only female in the whole store that dared try her hand at stocking. I only did it one night a week but that was plenty. It served its purpose. It kept me in shape and it provided me with some pretty kinky sexual experiences.

I remember one night in particular when I was stocking the top shelf in the oil aisle, the one we affectionately called Aisle 69. I was up on a step stool sliding some bottles of Wesson Oil back from the edge; that was all I could do to reach that far. I was wearing my usual stretch pants and store shirt. I was reaching as far back as I could when I suddenly felt a hand slip between my legs. It was that nasty fucker Bob, the one with the big cock and small mind who worked in the meat department. Go figure. I could feel Bob's finger press the fabric of my sweat pants in between my cunt lips. I didn't know whether to squeal and jump or moan and push my ass back towards him. I knew Bob was probably sporting a raging boner and after all, the store was empty and the surveillance cams were off until 5 am, so what the fuck. I chose to push my tight tomboyish ass back onto his hand. I could feel my huge nipples already hard in my bra as his fingers found my clit and started rubbing it back and forth through my sweats.

Bob was older and a big 'ole dork but never underestimate the power of a geek. In my 19 years of experience, well 5 years since I had been fucking, geeks always had knee hangers. I knew Bob was hung like a stallion and my pussy was screaming to be fucked by anything and everything. The more Bob fingered me, the puffier my brown lips were getting. I could feel them press hard against the fabric. I had fucked and played around with Bob numerous times and he was extra good at sucking my extra-long tan nipples too. He sucked them hard but then he'd twist my angry brown tits until I drenched my cunt so good it was trying to drip onto the shelves of aisle 69.

Bob had one of those cocks that wasn't exceptionally long, but when it got hard, the head was about the size of a bell pepper. It was always fun trying to squeeze that fucker inside my dark cunt, but once it was in there, man did it feel good. It was about the size of my fist, or at least it felt that way. I turned to Bob and yanked down my sweats exposing my cunt to his leering grin. My dark lips stuck out from all that dark hair and I couldn't help but reach down and stretch them out to their longest before letting them snap back into position. Bob had already unzipped his fly and pulled out Old Pepper's head, as I like to call him. Bob's hand barely went around his big ol' cock. When he got really turned on, it got bulbous and purple around the end. Since he had a cock that resembled a pepper one time I stuck a smaller pepper from the produce section up inside of my cunt hole. It made my lips pucker and bulge out around the outside of it. It looked nasty as it slowly emerged from inside of my cunt.

This particular night nasty Bob was in the mood to see me fuck all kinds of sundries from around the store. He brought me things from our infamous Aisle 69 and back and forth from the bottled pop section and the produce section. I loved sitting down on bottles of crystal springs bottled water that I made sure we're good and frozen. It felt like a massive cock stuffing your undies when you fucked that frozen clear cunt teaser. I also liked to fuck popsicles until they melted. Bob would get underneath me and lap the orange and cherry flavored juices up.

It wouldn't take long and Bobby boy would be smack dab under me, and I would end up riding the heck out of his bald head. I even loved rubbing my naughty clit button on his nose. I was humping Bob so hard that I almost didn't notice when I felt Bob pushing something into my ass hole. I turned around to see a polish sausage that was frozen rock hard going in and out of my ass. Bob was guiding it with his hand. I could feel my orgasm forming deep within my chasm.

I liked to let out all of the stops when I got close to creaming all up and down Aisle 69. If it could be fucked or at least attempted to be fucked it wasn't safe from my grasps. I loved showing old Bob what I was made of on the nights we worked so late. I was the wildest girl in the grocery store and I had a feeling I was going to keep that status for a while. Before the night was complete I had screwed bananas, cukes, sausages, weenies, water bottles, and even zucchinis. Right this moment I was in the middle of Aisle 69 giving a gourd everything I was worth and then some. Also, before this night of stocking was through I had successfully had 5 orgasms and my 6th was starting right now. I screamed and my orgasmic sounds reverberated all over the Sack and Bag. At the same time, Bob spewed his pepper head all over the canned vegetables and he and I laughed wondering what our next night of stocking would bring.

CHAPTER 3

BALLED IN THE BREAK ROOM (OFFICE SEX)

"C'MON, Eva. I gotta get this proposal done. I told you that earlier," Sam said. His voice was filled with annoyance.

"What I'd rather get done is *me*," Eva responded. Her dark eyes twinkled playfully at

Sam.

Sam's mouth quirked up at her joke despite his ire. "Yeah, I can tell," he said to the

young, pretty cleaning woman.

Eva began undoing the zipper of her cleaning uniform. Sam swallowed as a pink lacy bra came into view. Tan cleavage could be seen above the material. She'd been chasing him for two weeks and he'd resisted so far, but he didn't know how much longer he could hold out. It had been two months since he'd been with anyone and he was getting that itch big time. Eva seemed willing to scratch it.

Eva pressed her advantage when she saw the desire heat Sam's coffee-brown eyes. She pulled the top of the uniform down exposing more smooth skin and pretty shoulders. Sam felt his dick start to wake up as she shimmied out of the uniform and let it fall to the floor in his office. Eva crooked a finger at Sam and he rose as if in a trance.

He knew that he couldn't keep away from the sexy siren anymore and he didn't want to, either. She turned away from him, showing him her firm, shapely ass and the back of her supple, toned thighs. Then she ran away from him, laughing. Her long mahogany hair flew behind her.

"Catch me if you can!" she shouted.

"You're crazy!" Sam called back and started out after her. The girl could run.

He caught up with her in the break room. There was nowhere to run. She backed toward the wall and her eyes darted around as if she were trying to find an avenue of escape. Sam watched her sleek body move sensually as she inched her way to the right. The little scraps of clothing barely covered her private parts.

Sam lunged for Eva as she made her move and caught her around the waist. She laughed and struggled against him. Her body rubbed against Sam and ignited a high passion in him. He slid his hands over her smooth skin and his fingers snagged the shoulder straps of her bra. He pulled them down and exposed her breasts.

Sam felt like an animal had been awakened inside him and he captured one of her dark nipples in his mouth and sucked. Eva cried out, urging him on. It seemed that she was as hot as him. She raked her fingers through Sam's chestnut hair as hot surges of lust coursed their way through her body as Sam suckled her breasts.

His dick was growing hard and Sam undid his pants as he played with Eva's beautiful tits. His pants dropped onto the floor and he stepped out of him. Eva's eyes settled on his lengthening cock and she took a hold of it and began stroking it. His dick was smooth and hot and felt so good in her hand. Eva had wanted Sam since she'd started working for the law firm a couple of weeks ago and she set out to get him. Now she had him right where she wanted him.

Sam groaned as she worked him. He pushed her onto a table and made quick work of her thong. Her pussy was shaved and incredibly soft. Gently he spread her pussy lips and fingered her opening. She was starting to get wet and Sam spread the silky liquid up over her clit and rubbed her lightly.

Eva whimpered and started kissing Sam with abandon, letting herself get completely caught up in him. Her excitement grew as he played with her clit faster, his fingertips skimming over the sensitive bud. He broke their kiss and whispered in her ear, "You feel so good, so excited. Are you going to cum for me if I keep touching you like this?"

Eva nodded as sparks of desire kept pulsing in her cunt. "Do you want it faster?" Sam asked.

"Uh-huh. Yeah," Eva responded wrapping her arms around Sam's neck. "Please."

Sam stroked faster and pushed her legs wider with his other hand. "Do it, you horny bitch. Cum for me and make that pussy slick with your juice."

Eva loved Sam's dirty talk and felt her pussy start to cum. "I'm gonna cum for you, baby," she said.

"Yeah, do it for me. Cum," Sam ordered.

Eva's whimpers grew into loud cries as intense pleasure flowed through her. She felt her pussy grow very wet. Sam reveled in the dampness that covered his fingers as she came. He didn't give her time to rest. He slid his fingers inside her hot cunt and began thrusting hard.

"Oh, shit!" Eva cried. "Yes! Fuck it! Fuck my twat!"

Sam growled. "That's right. I'm gonna screw you silly," he promised.

Eva opened her legs as far as they would go as he continued to finger-fuck her. It felt so good. His experienced fingers rubbed over her G-spot again and again and soon she was on the brink of another orgasm. She couldn't hold still and moved her hips against his hand, mewling the whole time.

"Baby, baby! I'm cumming! Oh, fuck, I'm cumming!" she screamed as another huge wave of ecstasy washed over her.

"Your pussy feels so good," Sam said. "So tight and wet."

Eva smiled and put her legs down. She gripped Sam's hard cock and bent down to take it in her mouth. Sam sucked in his breath as she sucked and licked it. She had a wicked little tongue and seemed to really enjoy giving head. Eva felt Sam's cock harden even more and she wanted him inside her. She released him and lay back on the table.

"Put that big dick in my cunt," she said and put her legs up in the air.

Her pussy was pink and wet and Sam thought he'd never seen such a pretty pussy. He was happy to oblige her request and guided his ramrod stiff penis inside her tight twat. He pushed in as far as she would take him and drew out again. He did this several times, enjoying the feel of her satiny smooth sheath.

Eva thought she was going to go crazy if he didn't get things moving faster. "Please, Sam. Fuck it, baby."

Sam grabbed her thighs, pinning them against his chest, and began stroking her. He pounded at Eva, relishing the whimpers he extracted from her and the way her tits jiggled as they moved. A sweet tension built inside Eva as Sam moved in and out of her. She gripped the sides of the tables as the sensations intensified.

"Oh, yes, baby!" she said. "You feel so good!"

Sam grunted in assent and slammed into her again and again. His groin tightened and heat spread through his abdomen. Eva moaned as the pinnacle loomed closer. Suddenly she reached the summit and Sam plunged into her and tossed her over the edge. Pleasure flooded her body as she came and the sound of her shouts echoed off the walls of the otherwise empty break room.

"Sam! Shit!" Eva said as she shimmied against him in ecstasy.

A huge climax grasped Sam and squeezed him tight. His hold on Eva's thighs tightened and a growl emanated from him and became louder. Eva could feel his cum flooding her pussy and she loved it. Sam pumped several more times before coming to a gradual stop as his orgasm lessened. Eva smiled up at him and he smiled back.

"I'll never be able to come in here without thinking about this," Sam said. "Me, neither," Eva agreed and laughed.

Sam withdrew from her and helped her sit up. He gave her a long, slow kiss and then pulled back to find her smiling at him.

"This was so fun. I'll be back on Friday," she said as she began gathering up her underwear.

"I can't wait," Sam said.

"Well, you have a proposal to write and I have cleaning to do. I'll see you then," she said and gave him a little wave as she left.

Sam smiled to himself. An hour later, his proposal was done and he knew that it was thanks to Eva. He went home satisfied sexually and professionally and looked forward to his next night with Eva.

CHAPTER 4

ELEVATOR DELIGHT

I HELD my breath as his perfumed scent wafted towards me in the darkened space. I had always felt claustrophobic inside elevators, but now, I feel the odor of moistness between my thighs blend sensuously with his manly fragrance.

Andy was an officemate, but we didn't get past the "Hi" and "Hello" stage. We were both introverts, very shy, and had always retreated to the background during office parties.

I could hear his labored breathing, and the virgin lips of my pussy quivered as I could envision what his cock would look like.

"How long do you think the brownout would last?" he croaked almost inaudibly.

"Ummm, I don't know. This never happened before," my words hissed through my labored, lusty breathing.

I wanted to press my lips against his own and feel his phallus with my fingers. I closed my eyes and started rubbing my tits in the darkness. I could hear him hyperventilating. I had thought he was having claustrophobic problems as well. Who would like to be trapped in an elevator?

My undies were becoming wet with perspiration and vaginal juices. Then I felt something hard protruding into my legs. I instinctively moved away in surprise.

"I'm sorry," he said. "I can't help it."

I peered through the darkness and noticed that he had his pants down. An inexplicable thrill coursed through my body. I sensed my pussy quiver in excitement. Was he masturbating as well?

I groped for him in the dark, and my fingers stopped midway as his rock-hard dick found its way to my hands. He gasped as I enclosed his throbbing manhood with my hungry fingers. The contact heightened my need for him. I had to get his enormous, delicious cock inside me before the lights came on again.

Before I could make my first move, however, he was all over me, forcing his tongue into the moistness of my palate. His dick was already in my palms as I massaged it hungrily with my deft fingers. It became even more tumescent as he moaned with pleasure with my ministrations.

He grabbed my left tit through my half-opened blouse and rolled my nipple between his thumb and index finger, while he brought his tongue down on my right nipple. His action made me dizzy with pleasure. I never imagined the cool-looking dude next to my table was an expert in driving me mad with desire.

I wanted him to shove in his pulsating, huge dick into my willing pussy, so I moved my groin against him as my fingers increased their upward and downward movements. I was relishing his tongue with my hungry lips, tasting his sweet essence.

He gasped almost in pain when I nestled my hot, wet pussy against his manhood. We were standing, but this didn't prevent him from fulfilling his lust.

He lifted one of my silky thighs and shoved his big, throbbing, penis into my waiting love tunnel. I exclaimed in extreme joy as his shaft penetrated deeper, and deeper, with each of his powerful thrusts. I pushed against him as the elevator's wall provided support for my back.

We were half-naked as he feverishly thrust his dick into my slick pussy, and the elevator walls rattled and blended with our moans of delight. It was one of my sexual fantasies to be fucked wantonly in a standing position. The sensation was different because while he slid in and out of my tight vagina, his pubis also rubbed my clit adding one of the most pleasurable sensations I had ever experienced.

We sucked at each other's tongues and lips as his thrusts increased in intensity and my body was wracked with the pleasure of his angry, red dick. His dick went in and out, in and out, of my moist pussy, until our bodies exploded in a gigantic wave of delight that swept up our bodies in convulsions. I felt a little soreness, but I felt immensely satiated.

I could feel our love juices trickling down my legs, as we stayed glued to one another in our hips. There were voices coming from the outside of the enclosure. Soon, the electric current would be restored, and...

I shook my head as reality slowly seeped back into my consciousness. I hurriedly disentangled myself and searched in my bag for something to wipe the evidence of my lust. Thank God, I had wet wipes with me, enough to clean up and mask the smell of semen.

"Could... could I see you again, please?" he stuttered. "I'm Andy." "Of course, Andy. I'm Sandra."

We kissed once more in the darkness, as the lights came on.

He shyly looked at me as he straightened his shirt. I managed to comb my hair and assume a nonchalance I didn't feel.

The elevator hummed and within minutes, we were on the ground floor of the building. The throng of waiting for people crowded in as we pushed our way out. No one noticed something amiss.

We ended up laughing as we were left alone staring at one another in the car park. His mischievous smile told me he wanted something more. This was evidenced by the starting bulge visible underneath his slacks.

"What the heck," I thought.

"Where's your car?" I asked breathlessly.

We ran to his car excitedly, my pussy once more quivering with joy. It was like my first taste of ice cream and I couldn't get enough of it.

Inside his car, I discarded his shirt carelessly and pressed my breasts into his broad chest. He too was fumbling with the hook of my bra, but I slid it off when he could not unhook them with his trembling fingers. I knew then that it was also the first time for him.

I pushed him into the backseat, pulled his pants down, and knelt to take his already erect 9-inch dick into my mouth. I licked the crown and fondled its base and his balls as he threw his head back with a delightful groan. When I started going up and down his shaft with my tongue, it was too much for him to bear. In the cramped space of the car, he pulled down my panties and shoved my pussy onto his impatiently waiting dick.

The sensation of my pussy swallowing his dick was oh so deliciously exquisite; I bit lightly into his lower lip as pleasure after pleasure overcame me every time I slid my tight, moist vagina into his fiery phallus.

We hyperventilated as our passions controlled our movements and only his dick and my pussy existed in the universe. We clawed at each other, rammed into each other, as we moved and strained to reach our orgasms.

I rode him relentlessly, my luscious breasts jiggling, and my pussy sliding off and on his dick until I jerked upright and ground my pussy into his penis as my orgasms erupted in a kaleidoscope of sweet pleasures.

He locked his groin into mine as his orgasm overcame him too, and he grunted and collapsed against the backrest.

CHAPTER 5

SECURING THE GIG

THIS WAS her very first photoshoot, and Monica was beyond nervous. The photographer, Damon Hurt, had a reputation for being very hard on the models. From what she'd seen based on the last ten minutes she spent scrutinizing the other older more experienced models on the set, she realized that they were all afraid of Damon. The way he spoke, walked, and even glanced at them showed that he commanded authority and dominion over them. It was like a jungle and he was the lion.

When she caught Damon looking at her a wave of emotions rushed through her entire being. His intense gaze seemed to pierce through her very soul. Had she done something wrong? Why was he looking at her, with such a deep intense gaze? Monica didn't know but she felt the sudden urge to leave his presence. Running into one of the empty dressing rooms in the back, she locked herself in there. What had she gotten herself into?

Before coming here, she felt like she perhaps had modeling potential. However, once on the set, a new feeling seemed to sweep across her body. She felt foolish, like a foolish teenager. Gosh - she missed those teenage years, where she had no responsibilities, no rent, no bills, and no groceries. But now, at the age of twenty -four, with an apartment of her own, she needed to work to pay her bills. Modeling seemed easy enough, until now.

A light tapping on the door disturbed her thoughts. She slowly walked over to the door, with her heart racing. Who was at the door? As she opened the door, surprisingly she bumped into the man himself – Damon Hurt, the photographer. He was standing directly outside the door waiting. His body was warm and rock hard. A shiver rushed through her body as a little sensation ran from the middle of her spin and came crashing down between her legs. Monica looked up and his gaze fell into hers.

He was the epitome of what a man should be. A fine specimen of God's creation. She was shocked at the thoughts that were crossing her mind about Damon. He brushed past her and went into the room, ordering his assistant to give them a few minutes. Monica walked back into the room, curious to hear what he had to say.

"You're beautiful, you know that." His statement caught her off guard. Definitely not what she'd been expecting to hear from him at that moment. He took slow steady strides and walked around her, like a lion eyeing its prey.

A flushed feeling came across her features as his eyes carefully traveled up and down her beautiful body. Suddenly he wrapped his arms around her tiny waist and pulled her body closer to his.

"Damon!" she gasped as his tongue made contact with the nape of her neck. "I see you walking around here looking sexy as hell. You've been dominating this shoot, darling," his voice was husky and filled with desire. Monica wanted to resist him but it was hard – his body felt amazing against hers. In that moment, she found me for the first time, longing to feel his sweet caress. She was not a bisexual- she was just really aroused by this strikingly handsome man. A soft moan escaped her lips as his hand fondled her gorgeous breasts through the restrictions of the bra. Her body seemed to be warming up to his touch. He was without a doubt bringing about immense pleasure upon her. His fingers worked their way to the back of her bra and popped it open, releasing her perfect breasts; much to his satisfaction.

Bringing his eyes up to meet hers, he grinned a little and quickly captured one nipple with his hot wet lips. His kisses were soft and gentle as he used his fingers to pleasure her down below. Monica cooed, as his fingers slipped between the sheer fabrics of her underwear. The damp Monica between her inner thighs let him know just how aroused she was. Stroking the tender flesh lightly, he worked his finger over and around her swollen bud, while he flicked his tongue over her hardened nipple.

"Oh Damon!" she moaned breathlessly, throwing her head backward and trying to brace herself against the vanity table in the room. Using two fingers, he penetrated the heated slit of her core, thrusting them into her wet Monica repeatedly. As his fingers probed her insides, his sucking intensified, bringing about an imaginable amount of pleasure upon her. His breathing became sharp and heavy, as he began shoving his fingers into her temple of delight.

Suddenly he pulled away from her body and whipped out his cock. "How much do you want this job?" he asked with a serious look on his face. He stood there, with cock in his hand, waiting for her response.

"I don't want this job, I need this job," Monica replied, moving closer to him. She caught on to his game, and if sleeping with the photographer would lead to her success in the industry, she was ready to do it. She was not the first model to have done it, and she was sure she wouldn't be the last.

Taking his cock in her hand, she dropped down to her knees and slowly brought his raw meat into her mouth. Stroking it with her tongue, slowly she tried to maintain a firm gaze with him, watching his every reaction. Again, she took him into her mouth, sucking hard, making a loud slurping noise every time she released his cock from her mouth.

Damon groaned in satisfaction as he began slowly thrusting his cock into her mouth, enjoying the feel of her delicious tongue caressing his cock.

"Oh yeah...Baby suck it harder," he commanded his voice laced with desire in it.

Monica happily obliged, sucking onto his cock harder and harder, flicking her tongue on the head of his massive shaft occasionally. His body tensed up and his panting became heavier. He was quickly approaching his climax and she could tell.

"Come for me, Damon," she moaned, taking him in and out of her mouth, sucking his cock harder and faster while tightening the grip she had at the base with her hand. He increased the momentum of the thrusts he gave her, shoving his cock into her mouth recklessly.

Finally, with a loud groan, he exploded into her mouth. His sea of cum filled her mouth. Monica swallowed hard, taking a deep breath when she finished.

She pulled her lips away from him and shot him an intense stare. "Do I have the job now, Mr. Damon?"

"Oh baby, trust me you got more than the job," he replied, with a wicked little smile on his face.

CHAPTER 6

SEX SWEAT

WHEN JO FINISHED HER WORKOUT, the gym was almost deserted and that's just the way she liked it. She purposely always timed her workout to end when the place closed. That way she got her choice of machines and didn't have to deal with a lot of horseshit from guys.

Jo knew she was stacked. Her five-foot ten-inch frame came complete with toned thighs, tight ass, and killer rack. While she loved her body, it could draw her unwanted attention. A small price to pay, she mused as she showered. The hot spray poured over her curves and she wished that they were Eddie's hands instead.

Eddie Stratton, the owner of the gym, got her motor running and was the other reason she always timed her workouts towards the end of the night. Jo took every advantage to "run into" Eddie. Sparks of attraction had crackled between them in the past, but now Jo was ready to fan those sparks into roaring flames.

As she dressed, Jo let her jet-black hair fall around her shoulders. Her spaghetti-strap top was low cut and showed off her breasts. Her dark, exotic Asian eyes were entrancing and she knew it. She planned on using all of her assets to snare the hot gym owner and she was going to make it happen that night.

Eddie stood at the counter in the reception area, getting ready to lock up for the night when Jo stopped by. He took in her smoking hot body in her barely-there top and her faded jean shorts and smiled into her mysterious dark eyes.

"All done?" he asked. His gray eyes twinkled as he looked at her.

Jo nodded. "Yep. Well, there is one thing you could help me with," she said, "but you have to come over here." She smiled up at him. His blonde hair was tousled and she wanted to run her hands through it and intended to do just that and much more.

"Sure," Eddie said and came out from behind the counter.

Jo gave him a sly look and motioned for him to bend down a little. When he did, she grabbed his face and kissed him. He was surprised at first, but then slowly got into it. Stepping closer to him, Jo put her hands on his chest and ran her hands up around his muscular shoulders.

Eddie suddenly broke the kiss. "Are you sure about this?" he asked with an earnest expression on his face.

Jo gave him a smoldering look and said, "Fuck me, Eddie. Is that clear enough?"

Eddie laughed and said, "Yeah. That's clear enough."

Then he was all over Jo. He'd been watching her for weeks and when she'd started talking to him, he'd thought about what bad timing it had been since he was still with his girlfriend at the time. Then he and Rachel had broken up, but he hadn't been quite ready to make a move. Now, Jo was giving him the push he needed and he wasn't going to waste the opportunity.

He wrapped his arms around her waist and pulled her against him and then grabbed her ass and kneaded her firm cheeks through the denim. Jo opened her mouth to him, letting his tongue inside twirl around hers. She moaned into his mouth, hungry for more. She'd waited a long time for this and she was going to make the most of it.

She was surprised when Eddie picked her up and sat her on the counter and pushed his hips between her legs. He pushed her shirt up and started sucking on one of her dusky nipples while he played with the other one. Jo threw her head back and moaned as electric sensations coursed through her.

Jo tasted so good to Eddie as he licked and sucked her nipples. His gym shorts soon had a tent growing in them, as his dick got hard. He squeezed her tits and buried his face in them making Jo laugh. He smiled up at her and straightened.

"Lift up," he told her after unbuttoning her jeans shorts.

Jo's strong muscles brought her up off the counter long enough for Eddie to get her shorts and thong off. He noticed that the crotch of her thong was wet and raised an eyebrow at her.

Jo gave him a sultry smile. "Can I help it if you make me horny? If you weren't so fucking hot, that wouldn't happen."

"Is that so?" Eddie said as he ran a hand up one smooth thigh and stroked her

cunt.

"Uh-huh," Jo responded. "That feels so good. Don't stop," she said looking into

his eyes. "Fuck my pussy, Eddie."

Eddie found her slick and hot as he slid two fingers

inside her. Shit, she felt incredible. He began moving his hand, slowly at first but then harder and faster. Jo trembled and cried out as a powerful orgasm flowed through her.

After withdrawing his fingers, Eddie got rid of his shorts and a muscle shirt. Jo drank in the sight of his finely sculpted body and big cock and wanted him inside her desperately. She spread her legs wider as he came back to her. Eddie rubbed his cock against her soft pussy. He was so hard for her that it hurt. Slowly, he eased inside her cunt and groaned as her tight sheath closed around his shaft.

Jo wrapped her legs around his waist and kissed him as Eddie began pushing in and easing out. He was a fantastic kisser who gave her enough tongue without slobbering all over her. Eddie held her hips as he began pumping in earnest.

"Stroke your clit, Jo," he said. "I want to watch us make you cum together." "I like the way you think," Jo told him.

She barely touched her swollen clit and jerked at how sensitive it was. They both laughed and she did it again. This time she wasn't quite touchy and gently rubbed the little pleasure bud. As Eddie moved faster, so did Jo, and intense tension built inside her. Just when she thought she couldn't take anymore, an extremely pleasurable orgasm shook Jo.

"Oh, fuck! Eddie! Yeah! It's so good!" she shouted.

Eddie loved the way she moved as she came. When the orgasm subsided, Eddie grabbed her hand and sucked the pussy juice from her fingers.

"Mmmm. Damn that tastes so good," he said.

Jo angled a steamy look at him. "You like the way my pussy tastes?" "Oh, yeah," Eddie said and then slammed inside her.

"Yes! Oh, God! More, more!" Jo begged.

Eddie took hold of her hips and thrust inside of her over and over. Sweat began to make their bodies slick and Eddie's hair became damp as he fucked her. Jo came again as Eddie's cock hit her G-spot and she bit his shoulder and squealed her bliss.

Eddie's powerful muscles kept him pounding at her, driving him inside of her over and over. Jo was panting and sweat ran between her breasts. Eddie's dick felt so good as he stroked her and she wanted more. Eddie seemed to sense this and moved even faster. Suddenly, Jo was there on the threshold, moaning and clutching at Eddie.

Then she was coming and Eddie was coming with her. Eddie gave out a low roar as an incredibly intense orgasm rocked him. He felt Jo's pussy clench around him as she came, milking the cock of his cum. Several moments passed as they clung to each other in ecstasy.

"We got all sweaty," Eddie said with a smile at Jo.

She kissed him and said, "That's ok. I love sex sweat. Wanna work up some more tomorrow night?"

At home that night, Jo couldn't wait to see Eddie the next night and have a special "workout" with him again.

ABOUT THE AUTHOR

Helana Parkins is an emerging erotica author of many erotica kinks and sub-genres. Be sure to check out other books and leave a review if this story got you hot!

Visit my blog at Helana Parkins Blog

Join my newsletter for exclusive previews Helana Parkins Newsletter

Sign up for Free Stories from Xplicit Press Authors

Xplicit Press Author Updates

Like Xplicit Press on Facebook

Follow Xplicit Press on Twitter

Readers: I want to expand a few of the stories to see where the characters can be explored further. If there are any of the stories that you would like to read more about again, I'd love to hear from you!

Keep In Touch
Helana Parkins
info@helanaparkins.com